A Christmas Carol

Retold by Justine Korman and Ron Fontes

Illustrated by Lane Yerkes

inchworm
PRESS
™

Christmas was a merry time in London. But to Ebenezer Scrooge it was just another day, for Scrooge was greedy and mean. He was especially mean to his poor clerk, Bob Cratchit. Scrooge begrudged every lump of coal Cratchit used to heat his office. He paid Cratchit a tiny salary and grumbled about giving him Christmas Day off. To Scrooge, Christmas fuss and fun were just a lot of HUMBUG!

But one night something amazing happened. A ghost appeared. It was the ghost of Jacob Marley, who had been Scrooge's partner for many years. Marley had died seven years ago on Christmas Day, and he had been just as greedy and mean as Scrooge.

"You will be haunted by three spirits tonight," Marley said. "Heed their warnings or be doomed."

Sure enough, that night a spirit appeared—the Ghost of Christmas Past. He took Scrooge back to his boarding school days. Scrooge watched as his classmates headed home for Christmas. But one boy was left all alone at school. That boy was young Ebenezer Scrooge. Scrooge remembered how his father would not pay for the trip home.

Next the Spirit showed Scrooge a happier Christmas scene.

"It's Fezziwig's warehouse!" Scrooge cried. "I had my first job here. There's not a better man in London. Fezziwig treated us all like family. And what a Christmas party he threw! He didn't care about the cost."

Scrooge felt ashamed. He was nothing like Fezziwig. He'd never given Bob Cratchit a kind word, much less a party.

"My time grows short," said the Spirit, leading Scrooge to yet another Christmas from his past.

This time Scrooge saw the girl he had planned to marry. He watched as she spoke to a younger version of himself.

"You have a new love—money," she told the young Scrooge. "There is no room left in your heart for me."

Scrooge grabbed the ghost's robes. "Haunt me no more!" he begged.

Suddenly, Scrooge was back in his room. And the Ghost of Christmas Present appeared. This Spirit took Scrooge to a London street where even the poorest person was making merry.

"They are rich because they keep Christmas in their hearts," the Spirit explained.

Scrooge saw the cheerful Cratchits preparing their meager Christmas dinner. Though the plates were nearly empty, each dish was seasoned with love and good cheer.

The littlest Cratchit, Tiny Tim, was very sick. But no doctor had been to the house, for Bob Cratchit could not afford to pay for one.

Scrooge knew his own stinginess was to blame for the family's hunger and for Tiny Tim's bad health. "Will the boy live?" Scrooge asked the ghost.

The Spirit replied, "Unless the present is changed, the boy has no future."

Scrooge watched as Bob Cratchit lifted his glass, "A Merry Christmas to us all, and God bless us!" he cheered.

The family even drank a Christmas toast to Mr. Scrooge.

The old miser shuddered. Now he had seen how many kind people were hurt by his greed.

Scrooge was a changed man when he faced the final Spirit. "Ghost of the Future, I fear you most of all," he said. "But since I know you are here to do me good, lead on."

Scrooge heard two businessmen laughing. They were making cruel jokes about a man who had just died.

"I know these men. I've done business with them. Who has died? And why are they acting so coldly?" Scrooge asked the Spirit. But the Spirit did not answer.

Scrooge felt a great sadness. Was it possible for a person not to be loved at all?

"Surely someone in this city must mourn for this man!" he exclaimed. "Someone must have been touched by his passing."

Still the Spirit was silent.

Instead, the Spirit led Scrooge to the Cratchit home, which was greatly changed. Where there had been joy, now there was sorrow. For Tiny Tim had died. Though the small boy's life had been short, his death left a large emptiness. Many people mourned his passing.

Finally, the Spirit showed Scrooge the grave of the man no one loved. The name on the headstone was Ebenezer Scrooge.

Horrified, Scrooge grabbed the Spirit's robe. "Tell me I can change the things you've shown me! I promise to honor Christmas in my heart and keep it all year. Only tell me I can erase the name on this tombstone— and save Tiny Tim!"

Scrooge woke clutching his bedcurtains. He was alive! And he knew it was not too late to change the future. It was still Christmas morning.

Scrooge paid a boy to buy a huge turkey and deliver it to Bob Cratchit. "He won't have the slightest idea who has sent him a turkey twice the size of Tiny Tim!" Scrooge said to himself, smiling.

But it was true! And Scrooge didn't stop there. He made Bob Cratchit his partner and increased his pay. Finally the family had enough money for Tiny Tim's medicine, with plenty left over for food.

And Scrooge was right. Bob Cratchit was puzzled when the turkey arrived. "Only one man I know is rich enough to buy this turkey."

"Do you mean Mr. Scrooge?" Mrs. Cratchit said with a gasp.

The whole family laughed at the thought of the old miser sending such a generous gift.

   Scrooge became like a second father to Tiny Tim, and watched with delight as the boy grew strong and healthy. In time, Scrooge grew famous throughout London for his good deeds and kindness.

   For, after that night, no one kept Christmas in his heart better than Ebenezer Scrooge.